Fic
PEA

Pearson, Susan.

The spooky
sleepover.

65BT00886

$12.00

DATE			
mrks 99			

The Spooky Sleepover

The Spooky Sleepover

by **Susan Pearson**

illustrated by
Gioia Fiammenghi

SIMON & SCHUSTER BOOKS FOR YOUNG READERS

PUBLISHED BY SIMON & SCHUSTER

New York • London • Toronto • Sydney • Tokyo • Singapore

For Megan, greatest teenager on
the planet — SP

To my family — GF

SIMON & SCHUSTER BOOKS FOR YOUNG READERS
Simon & Schuster Building, Rockefeller Center, 1230 Avenue of the Americas, New York,
New York 10020. Text copyright © 1991 by Susan Pearson. Illustrations copyright © 1991
by Gioia Fiammenghi. All rights reserved including the right of reproduction in whole or
in part in any form. SIMON & SCHUSTER BOOKS FOR YOUNG READERS is a trademark of
Simon & Schuster.
Designed by Lucille Chomowicz
Manufactured in the United States of America.
10 9 8 7 6 5 4 3 2 1   (pbk) 10 9 8 7 6 5 4 3 2 1
Library of Congress Cataloging-in-Publication Data: Pearson, Susan. The spooky
sleepover / by Susan Pearson; illustrated by Gioia Fiammenghi. Summary: Two weeks
before Halloween Ernie invites three friends for her first sleepover, complete with
a feast, games, and ghost stories. [1. Sleepovers—Fiction.   2. Ghosts—Fiction.]
I. Fiammenghi, Gioia, ill.   II. Title.
PZ7.P323316Ean 1991   [E]—dc20   91-15773 CIP
ISBN: 0-671-74070-9   ISBN: 0-671-74069-5 (pbk)

CONTENTS

The Spooky Sleepover

CHAPTER 1

Almost Halloween

Ernie was excited. Tonight she was having her very first sleepover. The whole Martian Club was coming: William and R.T. and Michael.

First they would play Wizard's Woods. Then they would make popcorn balls. Then they would tell scary stories. Ernie shivered. Michael told the best scary stories. Even when she didn't believe them, they gave Ernie goose bumps.

"We should have a midnight feast, too," she told Daddy. He was helping her fix up her bedroom for the sleepover.

"Don't you think midnight is a little late for a feast?" said Daddy.

1

"But it's the spookiest time," said Ernie.

Daddy laughed. "I'm not so sure I want four spooked Martians running around the house all night," he said.

"We won't run around all night," Ernie promised. "Besides, it's almost Halloween."

Daddy pushed Ernie's bed up against the wall. "Halloween isn't for two more weeks yet," he said. "But how about this? We will set your clock ahead. When you have your feast, you can pretend it's midnight."

"Okay," said Ernie. "Can we have our midnight feast in here?"

"I don't see why not," said Daddy. "Give me a hand with these mattresses."

Ernie and Daddy pushed some mattresses into Ernie's bedroom. They spread them on the floor. Then they built a kind of tent over the mattresses. It was really just sheets draped over chairs and tacked to the wall, but it looked super.

Ernie turned off her bedroom light. She crawled into the tent. She turned on her flashlight. It was spooky already, and it was still afternoon. Ernie shivered. This was going to be the best sleepover ever!

Michael was the first Martian to arrive. He came in the front door. A gust of wind came in with him. A few leaves blew in, too.

"Looks like we're in for a storm tonight," said Daddy.

Ernie looked out the front door. The leaves were whooshing up the street. Except for leaves and wind, everything was strangely quiet. No kids around. No dogs barking. It wasn't dark yet, but it almost was. The birch trees in the front yard looked like skinny ghosts.

Suddenly, the streetlights flashed on. Ernie's tummy flip-flopped.

"Hooooooo," whistled Michael. "This is a night for witches!"

"It's not Halloween *yet*," said R.T. She and William were coming up the steps.

"Doesn't matter," said Michael. "Witches have to practice, don't they? And ghosts and goblins, too."

They had spaghetti for supper. "Worms 'n' blood," Michael called it. Then Daddy built a fire in the fireplace. Ernie spread out Wizard's Woods on the living room rug.

"I get to be the Wizard," said Michael.

"The Wizard is the cards, Michael," Ernie explained. "You have to be something else."

"The Spaceman, then," said Michael.

"No Spaceman, either," said Daddy. "How about Swift, the Silver Knight?"

"That'll be okay, I guess," said Michael. He picked up the figure of the Silver Knight. "His armor is good, and he has a nice sword."

William was Firefly, the Mystery Elf. R.T. was Princess Raina of the Forest. Ernie was Ilsa, the Magic Pony. And Daddy was King Leo. His playing piece was a lion.

"What will you be, Mommy?" asked Ernie. "Mirac, the Queen of the Fairies, is left. So is Web-Spinner, the Tale-Teller."

"I think I'll just be Mommy, the Popcorn Popper," said Mommy, and she went back into the kitchen. "Good luck, adventurers," she called over her shoulder. "The first pop-corn ball goes to the winner."

"So how do we play this?" asked William.

"The idea is to start here at Sheep's Meadow," said Daddy. He put King Leo on START. "And get to the Golden Palace first." He put his finger on FINISH. "But you have to go through Wizard's Woods to do it." He traced his finger along the path. "And you have to follow the directions on the Wizard cards." He stacked the cards, upside down, on their spot.

William started. He picked up a card and moved Firefly three spaces into Wizard's Woods. Then R.T. moved Princess Raina five spaces. Then it was Michael's turn. He picked up a card.

"The Wizard has put wings on your feet," he read. "Fly to the nearest toadstool."

Michael picked up Swift and flew him six spaces to the first toadstool. "Zoom!" he said. He loop-the-looped over Princess Raina. "It's a good night to fly. There's a storm in the forest. Listen to it."

The wind outside was blowing harder now. The trees were moaning. Branches scraped along the porch roof. Ernie shivered happily. It was a perfect night to play Wizard's Woods.

Soon they were all in the woods. Ernie imagined the trees creaking over their heads. She imagined elves under every toadstool. She imagined robins whispering secrets, and somewhere a wizard watching everything.

Then Swift got stuck in a cobweb and lost a turn.

"No cobweb is going to get me! said Michael. He pulled out Swift's tiny plastic sword. "Whoosh! Slash! Take that, and that!"

Ernie picked up a card. "A witch is after you," it said. "Run fast five spaces."

"Heh-heh-heh-heh," Michael cackled. "Run little pony, or the witch will get you."

Ilsa trotted fast down the path.

Trolls were following Princess Raina.

"*Shhh*," said William. "Be quiet and maybe they won't hear you."

6

Everyone began to whisper. The light from the fireplace flickered over the game board. Ilsa's mane glowed. Swift's armor shone. Wizard's Woods was filled with magic.

Princess Raina had escaped the trolls. Now she was lost in the fog. Swift was riding fast to her rescue.

"That is no ordinary fog," Michael said. "It's forest ghosts. Beware!"

Hooooooooooo, whistled the ghostly wind. Then pop! Everybody jumped.

"What was *that*?" whispered R.T.

"A ghost!" said Michael.

"A cannon!" said William.

Daddy chuckled. "There are no cannons in Wizard's Woods," he said. "That was just the fire popping."

Crash!

"*That* was no fire popping," said William.

Ernie jumped to her feet. She ran to the window. "Look!" she shouted.

The Martians and Daddy hurried to the window, too. An empty garbage can was blowing down the street. It banged and clattered. It crashed against tree trunks. It bounced over curbs.

"A ghost is riding inside that garbage can," Michael whispered.

The garbage can clattered on down the street. It looked alive. Ernie stared after it. Soon she could not hear it anymore. Then she could not see it. All she could hear was the wind. It howled louder. The trees groaned more. Then *plop . . . plop . . . plop . . . ploppety-ploppety-ploppety.* It began to rain.

Ernie looked at her arms. They were covered with goose bumps.

CHAPTER 2

The Ghost of Mrs. Maloney

A gentler popping sound was coming from the kitchen. Popcorn! The smell floated into the living room. Ernie's goose bumps faded.

"Let's eat!" shouted Michael.

"Let's make our midnight feast," said Ernie.

The Martians made a beeline for the kitchen.

"Is it time to make popcorn balls?" asked R.T.

"Not yet," said Mommy. "But you can fix your midnight feast. The water for the hot dogs is boiling."

The kitchen felt warm and safe and cozy.

No firelight flickered here. No sparks popped. Even the storm outside seemed quieter.

William stuffed hot dogs into a thermos bottle. Then he put the bottle in the sink. Mommy poured boiling water over the hot dogs and put the lid on the bottle.

"By the time you are ready to eat them, they will be cooked," she said.

"Got any catsup?" asked Michael.

"Sure," said Ernie. She took out a squeeze bottle from the refrigerator.

"Yum!" said Michael. "Boiled fingers dipped in blood!"

"And chocolate-covered ants," said R.T. She ran to Ernie's bedroom to get her backpack. She pulled out a bag of chocolate-covered raisins.

William and Ernie poured apple cider into another thermos.

"Witch's brew," said William.

"This is going to be some feast," said Ernie.

"All my favorite stuff," said William.

"Spooky stuff," said R.T. "It feels like Halloween already."

Suddenly, thunder crashed.

"It certainly sounds like Halloween," said Daddy.

A flash of lightning lit the sky outside the kitchen window.

"And looks like Halloween, too," said William.

"We're in for it tonight," said Daddy. "This is turning into quite a storm."

Everyone stood at the window and looked out into the dark night. Except when there was lightning, they could hardly see a thing. But they could hear a lot. The rain wasn't plopping anymore. It was pounding. The wind was howling.

"BOO!"

Ernie and R.T. jumped. *Clang!* Mommy dropped a pot lid on the floor. "Michael, you scared me half to death," she said. "Where did you come from?"

Michael laughed so hard, he had to hold his tummy. "I hid around the corner," he

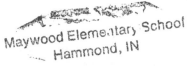

said. "You didn't see me disappear, did you? I fooled you all, didn't I?"

"You didn't fool me," said William. "I saw you leave. I knew you would do something."

Daddy plopped down into a chair. "Well, you sure fooled me," he said, laughing. "I was sure a ghost had gotten into the house."

"Maybe one did," Michael said in his spookiest voice. "Or maybe one lives here already and you just don't know about her yet."

"*Oooooh*," whispered R.T. "Maybe it's Mrs. Maloney."

"Who is Mrs. Maloney?" asked Ernie.

"She used to live here," R.T. explained.

"No, she didn't," said Ernie. "The Andersons used to live here."

"Before the Andersons," said Michael. "A long time ago. I never saw her, but Julia told me about her." Julia was Michael's big sister.

"Her husband was a river pilot," said R.T. "He drove barges down the Mississippi River. One day he started out on a trip, and he never came back. His barge just disappeared. No one ever found it. That's when Mrs. Maloney began acting weird."

"Oh, come on," said Ernie. "You are just making this up."

"No, she's not," said William. "I heard about Mrs. Maloney, too. Her yard was like a jungle. And she had twenty-five cats."

"Twenty-five weird cats." Michael lowered his voice to a whisper. "And then one day they all disappeared. All those cats and Mrs. Maloney, too. Poof! All gone. No one ever knew what happened to them."

"I don't believe any of this," said Ernie.

"It's all true," said Michael. "Mrs. Maloney was a witch. She flew away with her cats. Now she is a ghost witch. And she has come back to haunt this house."

Ernie turned to Daddy. "It's not true, is it?" she asked.

Daddy laughed. "Oh, there *was* a Mrs. Maloney," he said. "And she flew away, all right—on an *airplane*! Now she and her *three* cats live in Florida."

"That is what they *say*," said Michael, "so

people will buy this house. Her ghost is here, all right. Probably twenty-five ghost cats, too."

Mommy laughed then. "I don't think so, Michael," she said. "We have not seen or heard any ghosts since we moved in."

"That is because you have not been paying attention," said Michael. "Come with me. I'll show you."

Michael led them all into the living room. "Stand there," he said.

Everyone moved to where he was pointing. "It's colder there, isn't it?" said Michael. "Everyone knows that ghosts leave cold spots behind them."

Mommy laughed again. "It's colder here, all right, Michael," she said. "But the cold is coming from that window. That window doesn't fit tight. We haven't had time to fix it yet."

"You can't fix it," said Michael. "It will never fit tight, because Mrs. Maloney's ghost doesn't want it to fit tight."

Daddy ruffled Michael's hair. "I think I

will try to fix it, anyway," he said. "Next time you come over, Michael, there won't be any cold spot here."

Ernie hoped Daddy was right. She didn't want to live with Mrs. Maloney's ghost. Or with twenty-five ghost cats, either.

CHAPTER 3

The Ghost Cat

"I know how to prove Mrs. Maloney is in this house," said Michael. The Martians had returned to the kitchen. They were helping Mommy pop popcorn.

"How?" said Ernie.

"I will make her come out," said Michael. "If you see her, then you will believe she is here."

"You can't make a ghost come out, Michael," said William. "Ghosts are invisible."

"I know a way," said Michael.

"Then show us," said R.T.

"First I have to get the ghost room ready," said Michael. He was talking in his spooky voice again.

"We'll watch," said Ernie.

Michael shook his head. "You can't," he said. "It won't work if you watch." Then he disappeared around the kitchen corner. Ernie heard him in her bedroom. Then she thought she heard him in the den. But a moment later Michael was back in the kitchen.

"Ready," he said. "Now here is how we do it. First we count nine stars. Then we count nine bricks. Then we look into a dark room."

"That's silly, Michael," said R.T.

"No, it's not," said Michael. "I read it in a book. Honest."

"It won't work, I bet," said William. "Besides, how are we going to count nine stars? There are no stars out tonight."

Ernie didn't think it would work, either. It was probably just another one of Michael's tricks. But she did know where to find nine stars. "Follow me," she said. She led the Martians into the living room. She pulled Daddy's constellation book from the bookcase. "There are plenty of stars in here," she said.

She opened the book. The Martians counted nine stars. Then Ernie slammed the book shut so they wouldn't count too many.

"Now the bricks," said R.T.

"The fireplace!" said Michael.

The four friends counted nine bricks.

"And now the dark room," said Michael in his spookiest voice. "If you dare."

He led the Martians to the den. The door was shut. Michael flicked off the hall light. "It won't work if there is any light at all," he explained. "Are you ready?"

"Ready," whispered Ernie and R.T. and William.

Slowly, Michael opened the door. Ernie and R.T. and William froze. It *had* worked! There, standing by the window, was a ghostly white shape. They would never have seen it in the dark except for its head. Its head glowed. It seemed to be looking out the window. Was it really Mrs. Maloney?

Thunder rumbled outside the window. Then the Martians heard an eerie yowl.

Ernie jumped.

"Yikes!" shouted R.T. "Did you hear that?" She ran for the kitchen.

"It's Mrs. Maloney!" yelled William, and he ran after her.

"Her ghost cats are calling to her!" shouted Michael. He ran after them. "I told you I could do it! I told you I could prove Mrs. Maloney was in this house!"

Ernie's tummy flip-flopped. Goose bumps covered her arms. But she didn't run after the Martians. There was something very strange about this ghost. It didn't move—not even a wiggle. And its head was kind of flat.

Ernie took a deep breath. "I don't believe in ghosts," she said. "I don't believe in Mrs. Maloney." She reached inside the doorway. If this was a real ghost, it would disappear when she turned on the light. She flicked on the switch.

The ghost did not disappear. How could it? It was just an old sheet thrown over a floor lamp. A sheet from her tent. That Michael! He must have done this when he left the kitchen. Ernie pulled the sheet off the

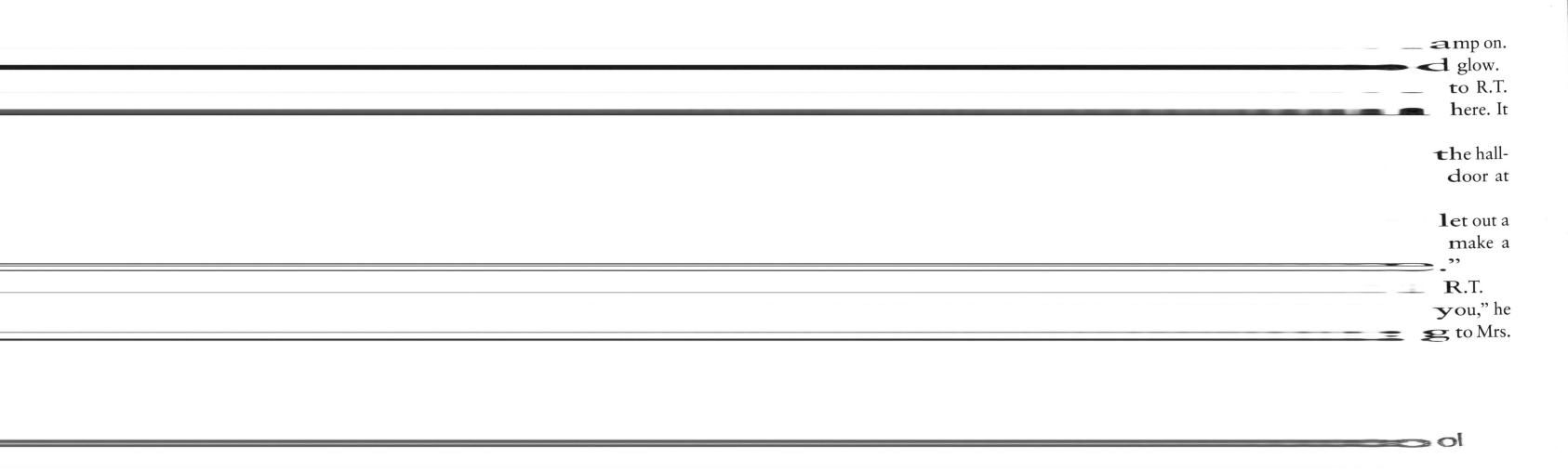

amp on.

glow.

to R.T.
here. It

the hall-
door at

let out a
make a
."
R.T.
you," he
g to Mrs.

ol

Mommy stuc...

bowl of popcor...

enough now," sh...

Martians."

Ernie and Wil...

stuck their ha...

Michael waved h...

face. "I'm a grea...

better watch out...

"Me, too!" s...

fingers.

"I am Mrs. M...

ted around the ki...

Ernie droppe...

I am Mrs. Maloney's cat," she said. "*Yo-o-o-wl* . . ."

William jumped. "Cut that out, Ernie. Mrs. Maloney's ghost cat may be listening."

"That was no ghost cat, William," said Ernie. "That was just a cat in the rain. Or maybe a dog."

"It was too a ghost cat," said Michael. "I was trying to make Mrs. Maloney appear. I got her ghost cat by mistake. Somebody must have counted ten stars or something."

"Nothing *appeared*, Michael," said Ernie. "Not Mrs. Maloney, and not her cat, either."

"That is because ghosts are invisible," said William. "You can't see them, but you can *hear* them sometimes." He shivered. "We made that ghost cat yowl."

"We sure did!" said Michael.

"*Brrr*," said R.T. "I hope that ghost cat goes away now."

"I think we are getting the stormy night jitters," said Mommy. "Wash your hands, Ernie. Then let's make these popcorn balls."

William popped some popcorn into his mouth. "Mmm."

"Yummers," said R.T.

"Don't *eat* it, you guys," said Michael. "Make it into balls."

"Let me into that stuff," said Daddy.

"Hey, Mr. Jones," said Michael. "Catch!" He threw his popcorn ball to Daddy. Soon there was a game of popcorn-ball catch going on in the kitchen.

"I bet we could bat these pretty far," said William. "Before they fell apart, I mean."

"We could try it with a wooden spoon," said Daddy.

Mommy laughed. "Not in my kitchen, you won't," she said.

"How about a juggling act, then?" said Daddy. He tossed three popcorn balls into the air and juggled them round and round.

"Too bad we didn't put in food coloring," said R.T. "Then they would look like real juggler's balls."

"I can juggle, too," said Michael. He tossed three balls into the air. He missed the catches. They all fell to the floor.

"Now look what you have started," said Mommy to Daddy.

Daddy bowed his head. He stuck out his bottom lip. "I'm sorry," he said. Everyone laughed.

Michael picked up his popcorn balls and tried again. This time only two balls fell on the floor.

Crash!

Michael dropped the third ball. "What was *that*?" he said.

"It wasn't thunder," said R.T.

"It came from the basement," said Ernie.

"The ghost cat," whispered William.

"Or Mrs. Maloney," said Michael in his spooky voice. "Maybe I really did it. Maybe she just appeared in the wrong place."

Daddy took a flashlight from a kitchen drawer. "I think I had better investigate," he said.

He walked over to the basement door. He switched on the basement light. He started down the stairs. Ernie and R.T. and William and Michael were right behind him.

"Don't walk so close, William," said R.T. "You keep bumping into me."

"Ouch," said Michael. "I stubbed my toe."

"*Shhh*," said Ernie.

Crash!

Ernie's tummy felt as if it had dropped into her shoes.

"That was thunder," said William. "Wasn't it?"

A second later the lights went out.

Ernie's heart pounded. The basement was pitch black. She couldn't see a thing. She didn't dare move.

"It sure is dark down there," whispered William.

"You can say that again," R.T. whispered back.

"It sure is dark down there," William whispered again.

Then Daddy turned on his flashlight. The Martians thundered down the rest of the stairs. They gathered in the light of the flashlight. Daddy aimed the beam around the basement.

"It's ghost light, all right," Michael whispered.

He was right. The light *was* ghostly. Nothing looked the same in it. Daddy's work

Maywood Elementary School
1001 165th Street
Hammond, IN 46324

counter looked like a spaceship control panel. His sawhorse looked like a jungle animal. The washer and drier looked like fat white ghosts.

Ernie shivered.

"*Brrr*," said William. "This place gives me the creeps."

The flashlight lit up a cobweb in the corner. The cobweb danced and glistened in the light.

"It's trying to catch someone," Michael whispered.

R.T. hugged herself. "I'm cold," she said.

Ernie felt cold, too. A lot colder than she usually felt in the basement. "*Shhh*," she said again. "I think I hear something." But all she heard was rain splattering and wind howling and a branch scraping against something. "It sounds as if the storm is right here in the basement," she said.

Just then Daddy's flashlight lit up a window. At least, it used to be a window. Now the glass from it was shattered on the floor. A branch stuck through the hole. Rain was splashing on the basement floor.

"That explains it," said Daddy. "The storm *is* right here in our basement. The wind must have blown that branch right through our window."

"That wasn't the wind, Mr. Jones," whispered Michael. "That was Mrs. Maloney. Now she really *is* inside this house."

"Oh, Michael," said Ernie. "You told us she was inside *before*."

"I made a mistake then," said Michael. "But I am not making a mistake now."

Daddy ruffled Michael's hair. "There are no ghosts here, kiddo. Now hold this flashlight steady for me while I clean up this mess."

Michael held the flashlight steady. Daddy swept the shattered glass into a pile. He pulled the branch all the way through the window and put it on the floor. He stuck a piece of cardboard against the window frame. He taped it to the frame.

"That ought to hold us for now," he said. "Come on, Martians. The excitement is over."

CHAPTER 5

The Midnight Feast

Mommy had lit candles in the kitchen. When they came upstairs, she was packing the midnight feast into the picnic basket. Ernie double-checked to make sure everything was there.

4 plates
4 cups
popcorn balls
chocolate-covered ants
witch's brew
boiled fingers
finger rolls
mustard and blood
12 big napkins

"Put on your pj's, Martians," said Mommy. "I'll fix up your tent and bring in your feast."

"Bring in a clock, too, please," said Ernie. "And make it say midnight."

Ernie and R.T. changed in the bathroom.

R.T. held a flashlight under her chin. Her face glowed red at the bottom and white at the top. "I am the ghost of Mrs. Maloney," she said.

Ernie giggled. "Why did you break our basement window, Mrs. Maloney?" she asked.

R.T. giggled, too. "To let in my cats," she said. "They are too short to reach the door-knob."

When they had changed and brushed their teeth, they went to Ernie's bedroom. William and Michael were already there. They had brushed their teeth in the kitchen. Michael had taken the tent apart to build his ghost. Now he was helping Mommy rebuild it. William was holding the flashlight. Mommy and Michael were tacking the sheet back onto the wall.

Ernie and R.T. unrolled the sleeping bags.

"All set?" Mommy asked. "There is a flashlight for each of you just in case you have to find the bathroom in the middle of the night."

"All set!" said the Martians.

"Good-night, then," said Mommy. "Enjoy your feast. Have sweet dreams." She kissed each of them on top of the head. Then she left. She shut the door behind her.

"Mmm," said Michael. "Boiled fingers dipped in blood. Mrs. Maloney's favorite."

"But not mine," said William. "Pass me the mustard."

Ernie poured witch's brew into the cups. R.T. opened the bag of chocolate-covered ants. William passed around the popcorn balls.

"Yuck," said R.T. "Those aren't the ones Michael was juggling, are they?

William shook his head. "These are clean popcorn balls," he said.

The clock on Ernie's desk said ten minutes after midnight. "I wish it was *really* midnight," said Michael. "I am sure we would see Mrs. Maloney then." He looked at William. "Ghosts become visible at midnight."

"I bet they don't," said William.

"We should stay awake and find out for sure," said R.T.

"Yeah!" said Michael. "Then we will have proof."

"Okay." Ernie agreed. She wanted proof, too—proof that there was no Mrs. Maloney ghost. And no cat ghosts, either. "But we will have to be quiet. Mommy and Daddy think it is too late for us to stay up until midnight."

"We can be quiet," said R.T.

"If I am too quiet, I will fall asleep," said William. "We have to do *something*."

"What, then?" asked Ernie.

"Tell ghost stories, of course," said Michael. "I'll start. Turn off your flashlights. Only the teller should have a flashlight on."

Ernie and R.T. and William turned off their flashlights. Now only Michael's light was on. He shone it around the room. He made it run up and down the walls. He shone it on Ernie's Cookie Monster poster. He shone it on Ellie and Teddy and Dina, sitting on Ernie's bed. He shone it on Harold, Ernie's pet rock. He shone it on top of her bookcase. That was where her milk carton village lived.

The village looked strange in the light of the flashlight. Bigger, somehow. More real. Mr. Frog stood in front of the library. Miss Mouse stood in front of Town Hall. The flashlight made them look almost alive.

"My village looks as if it is under a giant moon," said Ernie.

"This light is not moonlight," said Michael. "This light is ghost light. High above your village, a witch is flying. It is the ghost witch of Mrs. Maloney. She is aiming her laser beam straight at that village. Her twenty-five cats are hungry. She is looking for mice!"

"She can't have Miss Mouse," said Ernie.

"She can have anyone she wants," said Michael. "And now that she is in your house, she can have you, too."

The wind whooshed through the tree outside Ernie's window. It howled around the corner of the house. Far away, the thunder rumbled. Ernie shivered.

"That is what she does, you know," said Michael. He was using his spooky voice again. "She has been trying to get back to this house ever since she turned into a ghost. But the ghost cats keep getting hungry. They stop in houses and eat everyone inside." Michael made himself burp. "And now Mrs. Maloney and her cats are here. They will roast you in your own oven. They will sit at your table. They will sprinkle salt all over you. . . ."

Cre-e-e-e-e-e-e-ak.

Ernie's tummy fluttered to her feet. Goose bumps raced up her back.

"Here she co-o-o-o-o-m-m-m-m-m-e-s-s-s-s-s-s-," whispered Michael.

Ernie slipped inside her sleeping bag. She pulled up the zipper. "That was not Mrs. Maloney, Michael. That was just the house creaking. It does that sometimes. All houses do that."

"Not mine," said William. His teeth were chattering.

"That's the end of your turn, Michael," said R.T. She turned on her flashlight. "Now it's my turn to tell a story. And it won't be a Mrs. Maloney story, either."

CHAPTER 6

Great-great-great Aunt Ethel

"This is a story about my Great-great-great Aunt Ethel," R.T. began. "She was a pioneer woman. She lived in South Dakota in a place called the Badlands. Her house was made out of mud and stones and stuff. It had a dirt-and-grass roof. When it rained, it got very messy.

"Great-great-great Aunt Ethel didn't like the rain. That is why she liked the Badlands. It didn't rain much there.

"But ghosts don't like rain, either. They don't like water at all. If you want to get away from a ghost, just cross a river. The ghost won't follow you. So ghosts liked the

Badlands, too. There was ⌐⌐⌐⌐⌐
there at all.

"That was very bad for Gr⌐⌐⌐
Aunt Ethel. A bunch of ghosts n⌐⌐⌐
her. There was a mommy ghost a⌐⌐
ghost and a lot of itsy-bitsy bab⌐
There was a granny ghost and a g⌐
ghost, and a bunch of aunt and uncle g⌐
But Great-great-great Aunt Ethel never k⌐
it. As long as it stayed dry, those gho⌐
stayed happy and quiet."

"See, Michael," said William. "No ghost
came in the basement window tonight. No
ghost lives in Minnesota anywhere. There is
too much rain in Minnesota."

"And too many lakes," said Ernie. "Ten
thousand of them. No ghosts live here."

"That's what you think," said Michael.

"Let me tell my story," said R.T. Everyone
grew quiet again. R.T. went on.

"One day a huge, black cloud rolled over
the Badlands. It blocked out the sun. It was
like night all the time. Great-great-great
Aunt Ethel had to light candles all day long.

was running out of them. And her gar-
would not grow in the dark. She was
ning out of things to eat. She was in a lot
trouble. But the cloud would not move. It
ast stayed there and stayed there and stayed
here.

"First Great Aunty ran out of candles.
Then she ran out of food. She did not know
what to do. And then she had an idea! She
ran into her mud house. A bow and some
arrows were hanging on her wall. She took
them down. Then she went outside again.
She stood in the middle of her garden. She
aimed her arrow straight at that cloud. And
she shot it."

"Wow!" said Michael. "Did she hit it?"

R.T. nodded. "Yes, she did. And when she
hit it, that cloud opened up wide and the rain
came pouring down. It didn't fall in drops. It
fell in buckets. It rained and it rained and it
rained and it rained. Great Aunty's house
melted right there in front of her. One minute
it was a house. The next minute it was
mush."

"What about the ghosts?" breathed William.

"They were not happy anymore," said R.T. "They were very angry. And the person they were angry at was Great-great-great Aunt Ethel. They swooped up out of that falling-down house, and they were not quiet. They were yelling ghost yells. They were howling ghost howls. They were screaming ghost screams.

"They swooped right into Great Aunty's garden. They picked her right up off the ground. And no one ever saw her again."

"But what happened to her?" asked William. "Somebody must have found her again."

"No one ever did," said R.T. "She just disappeared."

"Like Mrs. Maloney," said Michael. "Maybe Aunty Ethel was a witch, too."

"She wasn't a witch, Michael," said R.T.

"How do you know all this if she just disappeared?" asked Ernie.

"Aunty Ethel kept a diary," said R.T. "She wrote in it every single day. And she was

writing in it when the ghosts carried her away. It must have dropped out of her pocket when they swooped her up. When the rain finally stopped, her friends came to look for her. All they found was a pile of mud and stones and grass, and a spinning wheel and a chest and a bed and a lamp and five more arrows, and her diary."

"*Ooooooh*," said William.

"That was a great story, R.T.," said Ernie.

"You'd better start keeping a diary, Ernie," said Michael. "Then we will know what happened to you when Mrs. Maloney gets you."

CHAPTER 7

Eagle-Ear Ernie

Now Ernie's clock said one o'clock. But that was not the real time. What time was it really? Ernie wondered. How much longer until midnight?

"We have to go look at the clock in the kitchen," she whispered, "or else we won't know when it is really midnight."

"Right," said Michael.

"Right," said R.T.

"Right," said William.

The Martians slipped out of their sleeping bags. They crept to the bedroom door. Ernie turned the doorknob softly. She eased the door open.

"Or Mrs. Maloney," whispered Michael.

R.T. hiccuped. Ernie's tummy flip-flopped. Then *Thump*! The Martians all jumped.

"What was *that*?"

"It's in the basement."

"Someone is inside this house."

"Let's get out of here!"

Ernie and R.T. and Michael and William dashed back to Ernie's bedroom. They dove into their sleeping bags. They pulled the zippers up tight.

"Whew!" said Michael. "That was a close call."

"What do you think it was?" asked R.T.

"Mrs. Maloney, of course," said Michael. "She probably tripped over something in the basement."

"That's silly," said William. "Ghosts don't trip over stuff. They pass right through it."

"Besides," said Ernie, "you heard Daddy. Mrs. Maloney lives in Florida."

"Then what made that thump?" asked R.T.

"I don't know," said Ernie. "I have an eagle eye. But I don't have an eagle ear."

"A burglar, maybe," said William. "Crawling in through the broken window."

Ernie shook her head. "That window is too small for a burglar to get through."

William shivered. "I don't want to think about this anymore." He yawned. "Let's read our palms instead."

"Neat-o!" said R.T. "Do you know how?"

William nodded. "My Aunt Dorinne taught me. Give me your hand."

R.T. held out her hand.

"This is your lifeline," said William. He traced a line across R.T.'s palm. "You will have a very long life, R.T. You will become a famous explorer. The first place you explore will be the Badlands in South Dakota. You will make a great discovery there. You will discover what happened to Great-great-great Aunt Ethel."

"Do mine next," said Ernie. She held out her hand.

"You will be a famous detective," said William. "You will have eighteen children. They will all have eagle eyes, just like you.

They will be detectives, too. They will detect the small things. You will detect the big things. Presidents from all the countries will ask you to solve their mysteries."

"Now me," said Michael.

William yawned again. "Hold out your hand," he said.

Michael shook his head. "I can do my own," he said. He looked at his hand. "Here is my lifeline. It goes right off the edge of my hand. That means it goes into outer space. I will be a famous space explorer. I will learn the secrets of the universe. I will be a Ghostbuster in space."

The wind rattled the windows. It whistled through the trees.

"Hear that?" said Michael. "The wind has a message from space. The wind is telling me to bust Mrs. Maloney. It is saying all this will happen."

"Now it's William's turn," said Ernie. "Hold out your hand, William. I will do yours."

But William had fallen asleep. So had R.T.

Ernie put the feast back into the picnic basket. Then she snuggled into her sleeping bag.

Michael was shining his flashlight on the tent roof. "This is our magic white cave," he whispered. "Like the one in Wizard's Woods. At midnight the Wizard will come. He will show me all his secrets. Presto! I will know the secrets of the universe!"

Ernie watched Michael's flashlight shining on the sheets. It did feel like they were inside a magic white cave. It would be a good thing if the Wizard came at midnight. Then he could give her an eagle ear. When she woke up, she would be Eagle-Eye *and* Eagle-Ear Ernie, World-Famous Detective.

Ernie's eyes were getting heavy. The clock on her desk ticktocked. The wind whistled. The rain pounded on the ground. But none of it felt scary now, not inside the white cave.

Ernie's eyes drooped. Before long, she was fast asleep.

CHAPTER 8

Martian Ghostbusters

Suddenly, Ernie was wide awake. Her heart was thumping. Her tummy was flopping. Her mouth felt very dry. Had she had a bad dream? Had the Wizard come? Had she heard something? What had woken her up? Ernie wasn't sure.

She wasn't the only one awake, though. Whatever it was had awakened them all.

"It came from the basement again," R.T. whispered.

"I thought it came from the living room," said William. "The burglar has come upstairs. He is stealing your silver, Ernie."

"We don't have any silver, William," Ernie

croaked. Her mouth felt even drier than before. "And if we did, it would not be in the living room." She opened the thermos of witch's brew. She poured herself a cup of it.

"It's Mrs. Maloney," said Michael. "She came in a spaceship. That's what made the noise that woke us all up — the spaceship landing." He peered out the window. "You can't see it now. That's because it's a ghost spaceship."

"*Shhh,*" said Ernie. "Maybe if we are quiet, we will hear it again." She hoped the Wizard had come while she was asleep. She hoped he had given her an eagle ear.

Everyone hushed and listened. The storm was quieter now. It was still raining, but there was no more thunder. The wind was softer, too. But her clock still ticked. The house still creaked.

"Come on, eagle ears," Ernie muttered to herself.

Tick-tick-tick-tick-tick . . . cre-e-e-e-e-ak . . . CRASH-CLATTER-CLATTER-CLAT-TER-CRASH! Ernie didn't need an eagle ear to hear that!

54

iptoed into the kitchen. The
topped now. The moon had
could see it through the
It made the kitchen glow.
light," whispered Michael,
stronger. That's because we
basement."
light, Michael," said Ernie.
ght."
st the same," said R.T.
flip-flopped. R.T. was right
s spooky. The counter tops
floor looked ghostly white.
ed as if it was grinning. The
re grinning back.
deep breath. Then she
he kitchen. She opened the
blast of cold air blew up to

ld where there are ghosts,"
d them.
ael," R.T. told him. "You
more than I am already

"What *is* it?" whispered R.T.

"It's in the basement," whispered William. He pulled his head inside his sleeping bag.

"It's Mrs. Maloney and her twenty-five cats!" said Michael.

"Or Great-great-great Aunt Ethel," said William. His voice sounded fuzzy through his sleeping bag.

"It is not a ghost," said Ernie. "There is no such thing as ghosts. Not in all this rain. And I am going to prove it." She crawled out of her sleeping bag. She grabbed her flashlight.

William's head poked out of his sleeping bag. "You can't go out there alone," he said. "I'm coming with you. I don't believe in rain ghosts, either."

"I'm coming, too," said Michael. "If it is Mrs. Maloney, I want to be there. I am the one who should bust her. I am the one who made her appear."

"I'm not staying here by myself," said R.T.

"Bring your flashlights, then," said Ernie.

"And something to fight with," said Michael. He took Ernie's plastic baseball bat from the corner.

at

He
po
sa

ful
up
th
wa

lig
It
di

po
he
"I

wa

"C

The Martians
rain had almost s
come out. They
kitchen window.
"More ghost
"and it's getting
are nearer to the
"It is not ghost
"It is just moonli
"It's spooky ju
Ernie's tummy
about that. It *wa*
looked blue. The
The toaster look
pots and pans we
Ernie took a
marched across
basement door.
meet her.
"It's always co
Michael reminde
"Stop it, Mich
are scaring me
scared."

Ernie held her breath. Was anything down there? She listened as hard as she could. All she could hear was her own heart beating. Ernie let out her breath. She wiped her sweaty hands on her pajamas. Then she started down the stairs.

CHAPTER 9

Ghost or No Ghost?

Ernie took the first step down. Then the second. *Cre-e-e-e-e-ak*. The third step squeaked. William was right behind her. His breath felt hot on Ernie's neck. Her hands felt clammy. But she was determined. Step, step, step—down she went into the cold and clammy basement.

"I can't see," whispered R.T.

"Turn on your flashlight, then," said Ernie.

CRASH-clatter-clatter-clatter. Ernie's heart jumped. But it was just R.T.'s flashlight bouncing down the basement steps.

"Sorry about that," R.T. whispered. "It slipped."

"*Shhh,*" said Ernie. "I have to listen." But there was no other sound to be heard.

At last they reached the bottom stair.

"We're here," whispered Michael. "Now what?"

Ernie aimed her flashlight at the window. The cardboard was gone. She lowered the flashlight. The cardboard was lying on the floor.

"Uh-oh," whispered William. "Something *did* get in. That was what woke us up."

"Maybe it got in before," whispered Michael. "When we heard that thump, remember? When we went to the kitchen to find out the time."

"You mean, it has been inside this house all that time?" asked R.T.

"Maybe," said Michael.

"Then why hasn't it done anything?" asked William.

Michael shrugged. "Ghosts are funny that way," he whispered. "They like to just hang around."

The Martians stood in the center of the

basement. They shone their flashlights into every corner. Cobwebs glistened. Laundry hung like ghosts. Daddy's saw grinned at them from the wall. But the basement was as silent as a school on Sunday. A chill ran up Ernie's back. The basement was as still as a graveyard.

Then Michael began to shout. "Come on out, Mrs. Maloney!" he yelled. "We know you're down here. I am the one who brought you here!"

"Shhh," whispered Ernie, but it was too late.

"Eeeeeek!" screamed R.T. "Something brushed right by my legs."

"Help!" shouted William. "It's here. It brushed by my legs, too!"

Ernie shone her flashlight around as fast as she could, but she didn't see a thing.

"Is it you, Mrs. Maloney?" shouted Michael.

Ernie listened as hard as she could. How could she practice her eagle ears with all this noise? Was there something on the stairs?

She wasn't sure. Then *cre-e-e-e-e-ak*. The third step squeaked. Ernie was sure of it.

"Come on!" she yelled. She raced back up the stairs. The Martians followed hot on her heels.

Ernie reached the top first. She stopped to catch her breath. The Martians clattered up the stairs behind her. They made so much noise, Ernie could not hear another thing. She shone her flashlight around the kitchen. There was nothing to see, either.

"Where is it?" asked William.

"Where did it go?" asked R.T.

"Nowhere," said Michael. "It is right here in this room. You just can't see it."

"We cannot find an invisible thing," said R.T. She shivered. "And I don't want to, anyway."

But Ernie wanted to find it. Ghost or no ghost? She had to know.

She shone her flashlight around the room. Daddy's wristwatch was lying on the table. She hadn't noticed it before. Now she could find out the real time.

Ernie picked it up. Her tummy flip-flopped three times. It was just the time she wanted it to be. It was midnight!

Ernie turned to Michael. "If it *is* a ghost," she said, "it is not invisible now."

CHAPTER 10

Ghost Jones

"We'll have to sneak up on it," whispered Michael. "Be quiet, everyone."

"And turn off your flashlights," whispered R.T. "I don't want it to see us, either."

"Come on," whispered Ernie. She tiptoed across the kitchen floor. The Martians followed right behind her. Would they see a ghost tonight? Ernie didn't think so. But they would see something, she thought.

Ernie stopped at the dining room door. "Shhh," she whispered. "I have to use my eagle ear." She listened carefully. Nothing. Not a peep.

Ernie tiptoed through the dining room.

She stopped again at the door to the hall. She cupped her hands behind her ears. She didn't need a wizard to give her eagle ears. She could give them to herself. She just had to pay attention.

She heard little wisps of wind. She heard a branch brush against the porch roof. And then she heard something else. Something different. It was a kind of splash. No, wait a minute. It was more like a slurp. It was very soft. If she had not been paying close attention, she never would have heard it at all. And it was coming from her bedroom!

Ernie tiptoed to her bedroom door. The Martians tiptoed right behind her. For once they were quiet. No one said a word.

The slurping was louder at the doorway. Ordinary ears could hear it now.

Ernie flicked on her flashlight. She shone it into her bedroom. She shone it right on the ghost.

The ghost meowed. Then it went back to drinking Ernie's apple cider.

"It's a kitten!" said R.T.

"Poor thing," said William. "It must have been out there in the storm."

"It crawled in through the basement window," said Ernie. "Look how wet it is."

"You'd better be careful," warned Michael. "It's probably one of Mrs. Maloney's cats."

"Oh, Michael," said Ernie. "Mrs. Maloney's cats live in Florida, with Mrs. Maloney." She tiptoed softly into her room. "Hello, kitty," she whispered. She sat down on a mattress and watched the kitten drink. Finally, it looked up.

Ernie patted her lap. "Come here, kitty," she said. The kitten shook itself. Then it looked at Ernie. Then it seemed to make up its mind. It padded over to her. It climbed into her lap. It began to purr.

"Oh, Ernie," said William. "It loves you already." The Martians were all in the bedroom now.

"It's so cute," said R.T.

"I guess it's not a ghost," said Michael. "It's after midnight now, and I can still see it."

"See what?" asked Mommy. She and Daddy were standing in the doorway.

"The ghost cat," said William. He giggled.

Then he and the Martians told Mommy and Daddy all about tracking the ghost in the basement.

Daddy laughed. "I knew we'd have four spooked Martians running around the house all night," he said.

"And now we have a new kitten, too," said Ernie.

"We'll have to try to find its owner," said Mommy.

"But if we can't, can I keep it?" asked Ernie.

Mommy nodded.

Ernie grinned. Nobody owned this kitten. She was sure of it.

"What are you going to name it, Ernie?" asked Michael.

Ernie looked at Michael. Her smile filled her face. "I'm going to name it Ghost. Ghost Michael Jones!"

Michael grinned. "That's okay if it's a boy

cat," he said. "If it's a girl cat, you'd better name it something else."

"Like what?" said Ernie.

"Mrs. Maloney would be a good name," said Michael.

Everyone laughed. Then Mommy opened the midnight feast basket. Daddy passed around the popcorn balls and chocolate-covered ants. And Ghost Michael–Mrs. Maloney Jones fell asleep on Ernie's lap.

"What *is* it?" whispered R.T.

"It's in the basement," whispered William. He pulled his head inside his sleeping bag.

"It's Mrs. Maloney and her twenty-five cats!" said Michael.

"Or Great-great-great Aunt Ethel," said William. His voice sounded fuzzy through his sleeping bag.

"It is not a ghost," said Ernie. "There is no such thing as ghosts. Not in all this rain. And I am going to prove it." She crawled out of her sleeping bag. She grabbed her flashlight.

William's head poked out of his sleeping bag. "You can't go out there alone," he said. "I'm coming with you. I don't believe in rain ghosts, either."

"I'm coming, too," said Michael. "If it is Mrs. Maloney, I want to be there. I am the one who should bust her. I am the one who made her appear."

"I'm not staying here by myself," said R.T.

"Bring your flashlights, then," said Ernie.

"And something to fight with," said Michael. He took Ernie's plastic baseball bat from the corner.

R.T. grabbed her slippers. "I'll throw these at it," she whispered.

William crawled out of his sleeping bag. He put on his bathrobe. He picked up some popcorn balls. "And I'll throw these," he said. He stuffed them into his pockets.

Ernie opened the bedroom door very carefully. She swept the light from her flashlight up and down the hall. There was nothing there, just silence. Too much silence. Why wasn't the thing making any noise now?

Ernie tiptoed into the dining room. Her light bounced off the glass in the cupboards. It bounced off the glass in the windows. The dining room seemed to shine.

"Ghost light," whispered Michael.

"What's that?" whispered William. He pointed toward the living room. Ernie aimed her flashlight where William was pointing. "It's just a chair," she whispered.

"*Whew!*" breathed William. "I thought it was a burglar. It looked alive."

Ernie aimed her flashlight into the kitchen. "Come on, Martians," she whispered.

The Martians tiptoed into the kitchen. The rain had almost stopped now. The moon had come out. They could see it through the kitchen window. It made the kitchen glow.

"More ghost light," whispered Michael, "and it's getting stronger. That's because we are nearer to the basement."

"It is not ghost light, Michael," said Ernie. "It is just moonlight."

"It's spooky just the same," said R.T.

Ernie's tummy flip-flopped. R.T. was right about that. It *was* spooky. The counter tops looked blue. The floor looked ghostly white. The toaster looked as if it was grinning. The pots and pans were grinning back.

Ernie took a deep breath. Then she marched across the kitchen. She opened the basement door. A blast of cold air blew up to meet her.

"It's always cold where there are ghosts," Michael reminded them.

"Stop it, Michael," R.T. told him. "You are scaring me more than I am already scared."